First Grade, Here I Come!

by D. J. Steinberg
illustrated by Tracy Bishop

Grosset & Dunlap
An Imprint of Penguin Random House

Dedicated to all first-grade teachers
everywhere, but especially Ms. McKenna,
Ms. Gingold, Mrs. Papernik,
and Morah Elana!—DJS

For Laura, Renée, and Christina.
Thank you for always supporting me—TB

GROSSET & DUNLAP
Penguin Young Readers Group
An Imprint of Penguin Random House LLC

Text copyright © 2016 by David Steinberg. Illustrations copyright © 2016 by Tracy Bishop. All rights reserved. Published by Grosset & Dunlap, an imprint of Penguin Random House LLC, 345 Hudson Street, New York, New York 10014. GROSSET & DUNLAP is a trademark of Penguin Random House LLC. Manufactured in China.

Library of Congress Cataloging-in-Publication Data is available.

ISBN 978-0-448-48920-9 (pbk)   10 9 8 7 6 5 4
ISBN 978-0-448-48921-6 (hc)   10 9 8 7 6 5 4 3 2

The Big Time

Eeny, meeny, miny, moe.
Once upon a year ago,
we were teeny-tiny small,
down the kindergarten hall.

See you later, kindergaters—
make way for the big first-graders!
Big-time backpacks on our backs,
skinny pencils, books in stacks,

desks to call our very own,
recess in the big-kid zone . . .
Time to read and write and add,
and fill our first-grade brains like mad,
till—*eeny, meeny, miny, moe!*—
we'll know the stuff that big kids know!

Pick a Book

Pick a book!
Pick a book!
Pick a book quick!
The librarian's waiting.
Which book will I pick?

This book looks fun, and it's for the right ages.
But *this one's* got dragons and five hundred pages!
I can only pick one!
Oh no, what to do?!
The librarian winks—
"Just this once, pick out two!"

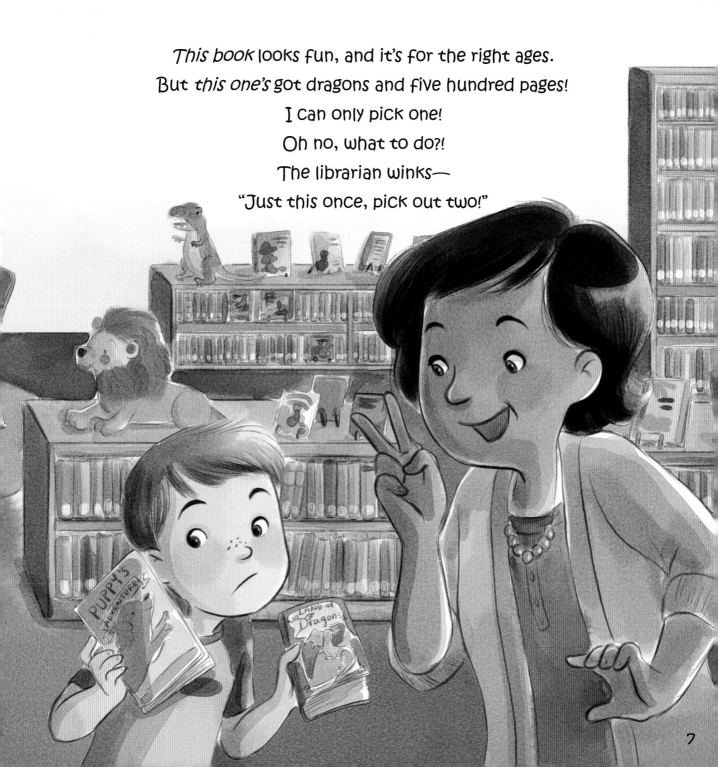

Spelling

Why do *t* and *h* make *th*?
Why do *p* and *h* make *fff*?
Who put the *w* in *write*?
Who put that *g* and *h* in *night*?
Do *c* and *h* belong in *schools*?
Who made up all these spelling rules?!

Math Problem

There are FOUR red candies
and THREE green candies
and ONE yellow candy on a plate.

How many TOTAL
candies on the plate?

ANSWER:
ZERO, 'cause I ate all EIGHT!

I Saw an Ape at School

I saw an ape at school today,
talking to a ghost.
And if that wasn't weird enough,
what freaked me out the most
was when a zombie shuffled up
and tried to take my snack.

Then—*wham!*—a wizard tackled him
and jumped right on his back.
"Attention!" called our teacher,
all dressed up like a queen.
"We still have work to do today,
even if it's Halloween!"

Is It Snack Time Yet?

"Is it snack time yet?" asks Austin,
first thing every day.
"Let's see," our teacher answers.
"What does the flow map say?"

"It's folder time," the class replies,
and so our day begins . . .
We put our backpacks on the hooks
and folders in the bins.

"Is it snack time *yet*?" asks Austin.
"What does the flow map say?"
We all recite the Pledge and then
check off the month and day.

"Is it snack time *now*?" asks Austin.
Not yet! It's counting time—
by fives and tens, and when that ends,
our teacher reads a rhyme.

"What's next?" says Ms. McKenna.
"Can anybody guess?"
"Uh . . . snack time?" mutters Austin.
The whole class answers, "YES!"

Smiley Face

I got my homework sheet back today,
which made my heart just stop—
in red it said 100%
with a big smiley face on top!

Birthday Cupcakes

Whoop-dee-doo—
it's Kendra's birthday.
She gets to lead the line.
She hands out sprinkle cupcakes
and wears the birthday sign.
Then everybody sings and claps—
I know I shouldn't whine,
but *happy-whoop-dee-birthday-doo—*
why can't today be *mine*?

You Get What You Get

"You get what you get, and you don't get upset."
That's what we like to say.
When I didn't get the cupcake I wanted,
we said it to *me* today.

BFF

Monday, Kim's my BFF.
Tuesday, I'm through with her.

Wednesday, we'll never be friends again ever,
and sorry we ever were!

Thursday, we kind of forget why we're mad
and how we started this war.

Friday, Kim's my BFF—
my best friend forever once more!

The Armpit King

Everyone loves Jacob
'cause he's the armpit king.
He sticks one hand inside his shirt
and makes his armpit *sing*.

What Did You Say?

I really was paying attention!
There are just all these thoughts in my head,
and while I was telling them all to get lost,
I didn't quite catch what you said!

Best Field Trip Ever

Today was the best field trip ever.
Our whole class was headed downtown.
We were halfway to some old museum
when somehow our school bus broke down.

The driver called into the station,
while we waved at cars on the road.
We got all the truck drivers honking.
Then the news came: "It has to be towed."

The teachers did not seem too happy,
but the kids—we were having a ball.
We all got to go get some ice cream,
and then we hung out at the mall.

When a second bus finally got there,
it was time to head back to school,
so we didn't see any T. rexes,
but, man—today's field trip was cool!

Pajama Day

Hurray! Hurray! Pajama Day!
Go to school the easy way.
Roll out of bed already dressed
in my flannel PJ best!
Slip my slippers on, no fuss,
and run outside to meet the bus . . .

Wait—why are they staring?
EEK!
Pajama Day's not till *next week!*

Money Fun

You can turn four quarters
into ten dimes,
then—*ta-da!*—twenty nickels . . .
how strange!

I love learning money—
you want to know why?
'Cause my dad lets me keep
all the change!

Anything Ball

We made up a game called Anything Ball
where anything goes—no rules at all!

Do you catch the ball, kick it, tag it, or hide?
Do you grab the ball, head it, or slide down the slide?
The whole class agreed that our game was *way* fun—
and the best was *both* sides decided *they* won!

Big Teeth

Check out that hole in Holly's mouth—
she lost *two teeth* last week!
Praveen's popped out this morning—
but me—I'm such a *freak*. . .
I want to be like all my friends.
I just don't think it's fair
that *they* all get to lose their teeth,
while *mine* are stuck in there!

LOST
TEETH

Holly   X X   X X
Praveen   X X
Andrew   X X X
Maya
Milo   X
Adelaide X X X X X X
Delia   X X X

Mother's Day

Can't wait till Mom sees her jewelry box.
She'll never know what hit her.
It's made out of paste and Popsicle sticks
and five hundred pounds of glitter!

School's Out!

School's out!
Summer's here!
We worked hard all year—
our brains must weigh half a ton!
And now that it's through,
I can tell you—
that first grade was awesomely *fun!*